A NOTE TO PARENTS

Disney's **First Readers Level 3** books were developed for children who have mastered many basic reading skills and are on the road to becoming competent and confident readers.

Disney's First Readers Level 3 books have more fully developed plots, introduce harder words, and use more complex sentence and paragraph structures than Level 2 books.

Reading is the single most important way a young person learns to enjoy reading. Give your child opportunities to read many different types of literature. Make books, magazines, and writing materials available to your child. Books that are of special interest to your child will motivate more reading and provide more enjoyment. Here are some additional tips to help you spend quality reading time with your child:

★ Promote thinking skills. Ask if your child liked the story or not and why. This is one of the best ways to learn if your child understood what he or she has read.

★ Continue to read aloud. No matter how old the child may be, or how proficient a reader, hearing a delightful story read aloud is still exciting and a very important part of becoming a more fluent reader.

★ Read together on a regular basis, and encourage your child to read to you often. Be a good teacher by being a good listener and audience!

★ Praise all reading efforts, no matter how small.

★ Try out the After-Reading Fun activities at the end of each book to enhance the skills your child has already learned.

Remember that early-reading experiences that you share with your child can help him or her to become a confident and successful reader later on!

— Patricia Koppman
Past President
International Reading Association

For Ted and Dan
—J.B.S.

First published by Disney Press, New York, New York.
This edition published by Scholastic Inc.,
90 Old Sherman Turnpike, Danbury, Connecticut 06816
by arrangement with Disney Licensed Publishing.

SCHOLASTIC and associated logos are trademarks of Scholastic Inc.

ISBN 0-7172-6461-0

Printed in the U.S.A.

HERCULES AND THE MINOTAUR'S MAZE

by Judith Bauer Stamper
Illustrated by Sol Studios

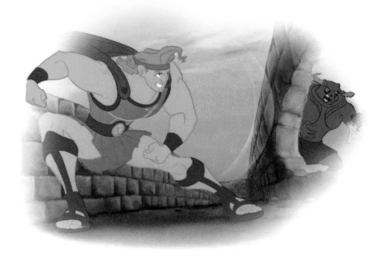

Disney's First Readers — Level 3
A Story from Disney's *Hercules*

SCHOLASTIC INC.

New York   Toronto   London   Auckland   Sydney
Mexico City   New Delhi   Hong Kong   Buenos Aires

Hercules was the most famous hero in all of Greece.

"Look at those muscles!" people said. That made Hercules blush.

"Under all those muscles is one shy guy," said his girlfriend, Meg.

Hades sat on a nearby mountain.

"Hercules really burns me up!" Hades said. "Why does he have all the fans?"

Hades snapped his fingers. The trees around him burst into flames.

"Pain, Panic!" Hades roared. "Get over here!"

Pain and Panic both ran to Hades. "Did you call, boss?" Panic asked.

"Is it hot here? Or is it just me?" Pain asked. He wore a Hercules T-shirt.

"Take off that T-shirt and listen!" Hades roared. "I have a job for you. And this time, we'll get rid of Hercules for good!"

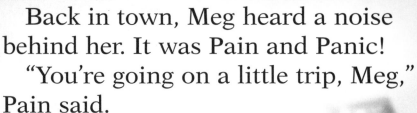

Back in town, Meg heard a noise behind her. It was Pain and Panic!

"You're going on a little trip, Meg," Pain said.

"Get lost, creeps!" Meg said. She tried to call out to Hercules. But it was too late.

The next day, Phil ran in with the mail.

"You have a postcard, Herc," Phil said. "It's from Crete, that place with the big maze."

"Crete!" Herc said. "A monster
lives there!"

"The monster called the Minotaur,"
Phil said.

"Who sent the card?" Herc asked,
taking the postcard from Phil.

"Meg! I've got to save her,"
Hercules yelled.
"Herc, that Minotaur is a mean dude,"
Phil said. "It's half-bull, half-man."
"Don't worry. I'm all muscle,"
Herc said.

"You will need to use your brains, too," Phil said. "In the Minotaur's maze, there is trouble at every turn!"

Herc hopped onto his flying horse, Pegasus. They flew off.

"There's Crete," Hercules said. "The maze is down there. And somewhere inside is Meg!"

Pegasus flew down into the maze.

In the maze Hercules remembered
Phil's warning—trouble at every turn!
Hercules turned the corner. A giant
lizard jumped out at him!
"Leaping lizards!" Hercules yelled.
He grabbed the lizard and threw it
over his shoulder.

At the next corner, Hercules ran right into the Minotaur! It charged toward Hercules.

Hercules backed up. He was trapped!

Herc heard Phil's voice in his head, "Use your brains!"

Hercules grabbed the monster's horns and flipped right over its back.

"Help!" a voice cried.
"I'm coming, Meg!" Hercules yelled.
She was in the maze. But where?
"Hercules!"

Meg's voice seemed to be coming from everywhere.

"I'm coming, Meg," Hercules yelled again.

Hercules turned the next corner of the maze. He fell into a pit of snakes!

Pain and Panic looked down at him.

"It's the pits, isn't it, Hercules?" Pain asked.

Hercules picked up two snakes and threw them. The snakes chased Pain and Panic away.

Hercules grabbed more snakes.
He made them into a ladder and
climbed out of the pit.

"Hercules, can you hear me?"
He heard Meg's voice again.
Hercules looked up at the tall walls
of the maze. He began to climb to the
top. Now Hercules could see Meg.

Hades sat nearby. "Stop him, boys," he told Pain and Panic.

Pain and Panic threw a rope. Hercules tripped. He fell to the floor of the maze.

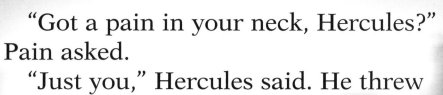

"Got a pain in your neck, Hercules?"
Pain asked.

"Just you," Hercules said. He threw
a lizard at Pain.

"Go away, you bully!"
Hercules heard Meg's voice again.
She was on the other side of the wall.
Hercules punched out a stone from
the wall.

He looked through the hole and saw
Meg. The Minotaur was charging at her.

Hercules pounded on the wall and the whole maze shook. But the wall didn't budge.

"My muscles aren't working," Herc said. "I will have to use my brains!"

Suddenly, Hercules whipped off his cape. He flashed it at the Minotaur through the hole in the wall.

The Minotaur turned away from
Meg. Hercules waved the cape again.
The Minotaur snorted fire. It pawed
the ground. Then, it charged!

Hercules waved the cape again.

The Minotaur got angry. It charged
at the cape. But its horns went straight
into the wall—and stuck.

"Bull's-eye!" Hercules roared.

Pegasus soared down from the sky.
Hercules and Meg jumped onto his back.
Then, they flew up out of the maze.
"Look," Meg said. "It is on fire."

"What do you know?" Herc said.
"I guess I was too hot for the Minotaur
to handle!"

Hercules and Meg landed safely
in town. Herc's fans cheered:
   "The Minotaur is beaten.
Meg is freed. Herc is our hero.
Yes, indeed!"

Enhance the reading experience with follow-up questions to help your child develop reading comprehension and increase his/her awareness of words.

Approach this with a sense of play. Make a game of having your child answer the questions. You do not need to ask all the questions at one time. Let these questions be fun discussions rather than a test. If your child doesn't have instant recall, encourage him/her to look back into the book to "research" the answers. You'll be modeling what good readers do and, at the same time, forging a sharing bond with your child.

HERCULES AND THE
MAZE OF THE MINOTAUR

1. **Where does the story take place?**

2. **What monster is half-bull and half-man?**

3. **Why is a maze a good hiding place?**

4. **Who is your hero? Why?**

5. **What does it mean when someone says, "That really burns me up!"?**

6. **Find ten verbs.**

Answers: 1. Greece. 2. Minotaur. 3. there are lots of turns, and it is difficult to find someone or something in a maze. 4. answers will vary. 5. it means, "That makes me angry!" 6. *possible answers:* heard, hopped, flew, jumped, grabbed, threw, stomped, charged, flipped, and yelled.